Hidden Sky

by Lilly Trcka

illustrations by
Jacqueline Paske Gill

*Dedicated to my family~
thanks for everything.

ISBN-13: 978-1984086792
ISBN-10: 1984086790

Printed in the U.S.A.

You never know what you might find when you're having fun.
That's what Sam learns while playing a simple game of hide and seek.
What he discovers will change his world forever.

Sam sprinted for the bushes. "Eight, nine...."
Danny's voice faded away as Sam dove into the
bushes. He huddled in a ball, grinning. Danny
would never find him here!

Then he heard a rustling sound in front of him. Sam gasped in shock as two large sky blue eyes appeared, looking at him from the shadows. "Who.. Who are you?" Sam breathed. The eyes regarded him warily.

Then a large dog slid out of the shadows. In the distance Sam heard Danny yell, "Thirty! Ready or not, here I come!" But Sam's attention was fixed on the dog. He was a soft gray with patches of black on his coat. He looked like the night sky with his dark fur and his blue eyes. "Whoa," Sam whispered. The dog was thin and dirty with mud. But he was the most beautiful thing Sam had ever seen. Sam noticed there was no collar around his neck.

Sam held out his hand. The dog looked at it, and then sniffed it. He licked it. At that moment Sam decided then and forever that this dog would be his, no matter what his parents would say. "Sky," Sam smiled. The dog looked up at him and barked softly.

Sam got up and began to walk, calling the dog, "Come Sky! Come!" Sky gazed after the nine year old boy. His ear twitched. "Fine, Sky," Sam sighed, "stay, boy, stay!"

He hurried home, not meeting Danny or any of the other boys playing hide-and-seek. When he got close enough to the house, he saw Sky waiting for him. Sam grinned. Sky was one amazing dog! Sam ran up to him and petted him. Sky flinched, but then relaxed. Sam told him, "I'll be right back, buddy."

He ran up the stone steps and hurried into the house. "Mom, Dad!" he called. "Sam?" Mom appeared at the end of the hallway, Dad right behind her. "There's this super amazing dog outside!" Sam cried, "Come and meet him!" Mom and Dad glanced at each other.

"Sure, honey," Mom said, a smile on her face.

Sam dashed back outside. Sky was still sitting there. Mom and Dad followed him and both gasped at the same time.

"Can we keep him? Please?" Sam went to stand by Sky's side. "I don't know Sam," Dad's eyes traveled over Sky's dirty, tangled fur.

"Pleeeaaase! He can have Jammin's old dish and toys!" Sam gazed at his parents pleadingly.

Mom winced. Jammin had been their last dog, and she had to be put down about three weeks ago because she had cancer.

Mom and Dad looked at each other. "All right,"
Mom sighed. "Yay!" Sam hugged Sky's neck.
Sky licked his arm. "You're our dog now, Sky!"

Made in the USA
Lexington, KY
23 May 2018